Jungle Adventure

Adapted by Cathy Hapka

SCHOLASTIC INC.

ISBN 978-0-545-79410-7

10 9 8 7 6 5 4 3 2 1   15 16 17 18 19 20/0

Printed in the U.S.A.   40
First printing, January 2015

Table of Contents

Chapter 1: Wedding Plans

"You look stunning, Aunt Sophie!" Olivia exclaimed.

"So cosmopolitan," Stephanie added.

Olivia's aunt gazed at herself in the bridal shop mirror. "I don't know," she said. "I'm not sure I'm the cosmopolitan type."

Olivia and her four best friends, Stephanie, Andrea, Emma, and Mia, were helping Olivia's aunt, Sophie, plan her wedding. Sophie was the head veterinarian at the Heartlake Vet Clinic. She was marrying Henry, a man she'd met years

earlier in vet school. Henry had invited Sophie to come to the jungle and help him with the Animal Rescue Station he'd started there. Soon after that, the two of them had become best friends, and before long, they'd fallen in love. Olivia could hardly believe the wedding was only a few short weeks away!

Andrea stepped forward to show Sophie the screen of her smartphone. "Any of these accessories would fit the dress perfectly," she said.

"And we'll use just the right flowers to complete the look," Emma chimed in.

"Oh, girls," Sophie said with a smile. "I'm so glad you're helping me plan the wedding! Especially since Henry's busy at the Animal Rescue Station this week."

"Don't worry, Aunt Sophie," Olivia said. "We'll make sure everything is perfect!"

Olivia was positive that she and her friends were up to the task. Emma knew just the right way to make any outfit, especially a bridal ensemble, look stunning. Andrea was full of energy and fun ideas. Stephanie was terrific at planning events, big or small. And Mia, well, she loved animals just as much as Sophie and Henry. She was certain to make sure the bride's and groom's personalities were expressed perfectly in the wedding details.

As for Olivia, she just wanted her aunt to be happy.

Sophie went into the dressing room to try on another gown. While she was gone, Olivia's cell phone rang. It was Henry's nephew, Matthew. He

was helping Henry at the Animal Rescue Station in the jungle that week.

"Hey, Matthew!" Olivia said brightly. "How are things going?"

"I don't want to worry Sophie." Matthew's

voice sounded fuzzy through the static on the line. "But Uncle Henry didn't check in last night."

"What?" Olivia exclaimed. "Are you telling me that the groom is missing in the jungle?"

She gasped at the thought. The Animal Rescue Station was located deep in the jungle. She had been there before, and it definitely wasn't the kind of place where she would ever want to get lost!

"No, no, not at all," Matthew said quickly. "Henry sometimes stays out for more than one day. He usually takes extra food—"

"'Sometimes' and 'usually' aren't good enough, Matthew," Olivia interrupted. "This is your uncle and my future uncle we're talking about! Henry wouldn't do this so close to the wedding. Can you go look for him?"

"I have to stay with the animals," Matthew said. "I'm the only one here."

"Then I'll be on the way soon." Olivia hung up and waved her friends over. She quickly told them what Henry had told her.

"What should we do?" Mia asked quietly so Sophie wouldn't hear.

"I have to go find him," Olivia said. "I've been out there before so I know my way around." She paused. "A little."

"I'll go with you," Mia said.

Stephanie nodded. "Me, too!"

"Emma and I will stay with Sophie," Andrea said. "We can keep working on wedding plans while you're gone."

"Okay," Olivia said. "But don't tell her where we are. I don't want her to worry."

Emma smiled. "The secret's safe with us," she promised.

Chapter 2:
Spa Secrets

Olivia, Mia, and Stephanie packed and took flight in Stephanie's plane for the jungle that very afternoon. Meanwhile, Andrea was thinking about her friends' mission as she hurried toward a local spa. She was supposed to meet Emma and Sophie there for facials. Actually, Olivia was the one who had organized the spa appointment. What was Andrea going to tell Sophie when she asked why Olivia wasn't there?

Sophie was waiting just outside. Andrea gave her a big smile and ushered the bride-to-be into the lobby of the spa.

"Sophie, you're going to love this day spa!" she exclaimed. "Your skin will look amazing."

"Sounds great, Andrea," Aunt Sophie said. "Where's Olivia?"

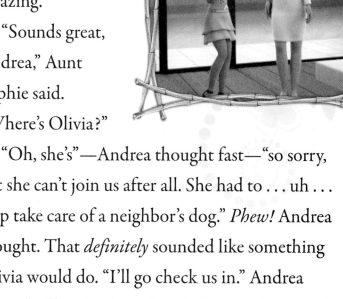

"Oh, she's"—Andrea thought fast—"so sorry, but she can't join us after all. She had to . . . uh . . . help take care of a neighbor's dog." *Phew!* Andrea thought. That *definitely* sounded like something Olivia would do. "I'll go check us in." Andrea hurried off to the front desk before Sophie could ask any more questions.

Just then, Emma raced in, out of breath. "Sorry I'm late!" she said to Sophie. "I hate to tell you this, but Olivia just called me. She has to spend the rest of the day in the library studying for a test. So she can't make it."

Sophie's eyes narrowed slightly. "Oh, really?" she asked. She glanced from Emma to Andrea and back again.

Something suspicious was going on.

Meanwhile, Olivia was in the passenger seat of a sturdy all-terrain vehicle bouncing through the jungle. Matthew was driving, and Stephanie and Mia were in the backseat. The road was bumpy and rough, pockmarked with ruts and mud puddles. But the jungle was amazing!

Olivia only wished that she wasn't too worried to enjoy it. Matthew still hadn't heard any word from Henry.

"Wow," Mia said, holding on as the vehicle tossed back and forth. "It's beautiful here!"

Stephanie, however, seemed distracted. "Oh, no!" she cried. "My phone has no signal! This is a disaster! We have to go back!"

The other girls giggled. If there was one thing Stephanie hated, it was feeling disconnected from the outside world.

"This is what we use out here," Matthew said, handing Stephanie a radio walkie-talkie.

Stephanie took it, though she looked dubious. "No calendar function or messaging," she murmured. "But it seems durable. Great battery life, too. Okay, it'll do. I'll check in with Andrea."

Back at the spa, Andrea, Emma, and Sophie were in the middle of getting their mud mask facials. An employee smiled at Sophie.

"Why don't we do your pedicure while your mud mask dries?" the woman suggested.

"Bye, girls." Sophie waved.

"So far so good," Emma whispered to Andrea the moment Sophie was out of earshot. "She totally believed me when I told her Olivia had to study at the library all day."

"You told her that?" Andrea exclaimed. "But I already told her Olivia had to take care of a neighbor's dog!"

Emma gasped. "Oh, no!"

"Okay, girls." Another spa employee came over, holding a bowl filled with mud-mask cream. "No more talking. You don't want to crack your masks."

As the woman applied the girls' mud masks, Andrea's phone buzzed.

"Sorry," Andrea said. "I have to answer this."

Andrea turned on her phone's speaker function so she wouldn't have to hold it too close to her face. It was Stephanie calling!

"How's it going?" Stephanie's voice came over the speaker, crackling with static.

"Fine," Andrea replied, trying not to move her lips so she wouldn't ruin her mask. "We're getting mud masks."

"You're getting mermasks?" Stephanie asked. "What's that?"

"Mud. Masks," Andrea repeated. It wasn't easy to speak without moving her lips!

"Oh, nice," Stephanie said. "We're on our way to base camp."

"Space camp?" Andrea almost wrinkled her nose in confusion, but caught herself in time. "I thought you were in the jungle?"

"We are!" Stephanie exclaimed.

"Okay," Andrea replied. "Just tell Olivia that Sophie doesn't suspect a thing about Henry. I have to go. Bye."

As Andrea hung up, a stern voice suddenly asked, "What about Henry? Who were you talking to?"

Whoops! Sophie had come back just in time to hear the end of Andrea's conversation!

"Okay, spill it, girls," Sophie insisted. "Now."

"Easy, Sophie," Emma said. "You'll crack your—"

CRRRACK!

Sophie's mask cracked. But she didn't even seem to notice.

Chapter 3: Welcome to the Jungle

"Here we are!" Matthew said as he stopped the jeep at the jungle base camp. Stephanie hardly knew what to look at first! The camp was built right amidst the trees. Monkeys swung from branch to branch, and colorful birds flitted through the treetops.

As Matthew and the girls climbed out, a baby panda scampered over and nuzzled Stephanie's leg. She picked him up.

"Aw, hey, little guy!" she exclaimed.

"That's Shadow," Matthew said.

"He's *soooo* cute!" Stephanie cooed, nuzzling the panda.

"His brother, Bamboo, is out here somewhere, too," Matthew told the girls. "We were only able to rescue Shadow so far."

"Aw, I bet you miss your brother, huh, Shadow?" Mia gave the panda cub a gentle pat.

"We can play with Shadow later," Olivia said. "We've got to search for Henry."

"It's too late today," Matthew said. "It'll be dark soon. You'll have to wait until morning."

Stephanie knew Matthew was right, but she felt impatient and restless. Luckily, she didn't have to look far for something to distract her.

"This place is a mess," she declared. Buckets and supply crates were scattered everywhere. "Look at all this stuff! Maybe Henry's been here all along but we just can't see him behind all the clutter."

"Very funny," Matthew said. "But it's no use cleaning up, Stephanie."

"Sorry, Matthew," Stephanie said with a wave of her hand. "Those words don't register with me!"

She started to tidy up the kitchen area. Suddenly, she heard a loud clanging sound. A monkey ran past holding a frying pan and a metal spoon!

"Give me that!" Stephanie cried, chasing the monkey. "Those don't belong to you!"

Matthew shook his head. "I told her it was no use cleaning up."

"Don't you think it's odd that Henry hasn't checked in?" Olivia asked him.

"It's possible his walkie-talkie isn't working and he's just fine," Matthew replied. "These sorts of things happen in the jungle. You didn't have to rush all the way out here."

Just then, something caught Olivia's eye. It was a brightly colored parrot. It flew past and landed atop one of the base camp buildings.

"I may know one reason Henry might not have checked in," Olivia said, pointing. "Look, there's a

nest on top of the antenna!"

Matthew's eyes grew wide. "Oh, I didn't see that before! I'll go get the ladder."

Olivia knew a lot about technology. With a bird's nest blocking the signal, walkie-talkie messages might not be able to make it through to the base camp. Maybe if they moved the nest, they would get a message from Henry!

The friends got to work. Matthew brought a ladder, and Olivia climbed up to the antenna.

"Careful not to touch the eggs," Mia called up to her. "We don't want the mother parrot to reject them."

Olivia carefully shifted the nest over onto a large crook in the tree closest to the antenna. "Sorry I had to move your family," she told the mother parrot. "But I think you'll like this spot much better."

As Olivia climbed down, Matthew's walkie-talkie crackled to life. Henry's voice came through! But the transmission sounded extra garbled. They could only understand a few words of what he was saying.

"... at D-mon Falls ... tell Sophie ... over."

The transmission cut off. Olivia punched a button on the walkie-talkie.

"Henry?" she said loudly. "Come in, Henry. Over!"

Everyone held their breath and waited. But there was no response.

"Well, at least we know where he is now," Matthew said. "Demon Falls."

"Demon Falls?" Mia shivered. "That doesn't sound like the kind of place you'd want to hike!"

Still, as soon as morning came the girls

prepared to set out. Matthew had to stay behind because he was the only one who knew how to take care of the rescued animals. He gave the friends a walkie-talkie and a map.

"Just call if you get into any trouble," he said.

Mia rolled her eyes. "Traveling to a creepy-sounding place like Demon Falls, what could possibly happen?"

"We'll be fine," Olivia assured Matthew. "We'll be back soon with Henry."

Chapter 4:
Wild Surprises

Olivia confidently led the way through the jungle, consulting her map at every twist and turn. Finally, she declared, "Here we are, you guys! Demon Falls should be right . . . here."

The girls stepped forward into a clearing and frowned. This didn't look like Demon Falls at all. In fact . . .

"Demon Falls sure looks a lot like base camp," Mia said sarcastically.

"Oh, no!" Olivia's shoulders slumped. "We went in a circle!"

"Maybe I should navigate." Stephanie reached for the map.

But Olivia pulled it away. "No, I've got this," she said. "Really. I think I know where we went wrong."

They set out again. This time Olivia led them to the bank of a river.

"This river is on the map," she said. "So I know we're heading in the right direction."

She took a few more steps. Suddenly she heard a twig snap loudly in the underbrush up ahead. Olivia froze.

"*Shh!*" she warned her friends. "I think it's a wild animal. On three, we jump out, scream, and wave our arms to scare it away. One, two, three!"

Olivia, Stephanie, and Mia leaped forward. They all screamed at the tops of their lungs while waving their arms wildly!

There was a frightened scream in return. It sounded familiar . . .

Olivia gasped as she realized there was no wild animal. Instead, Andrea, Emma, and Sophie popped out from the underbrush!

"It's you guys!" Mia exclaimed.

"What a relief!" Olivia cried, hugging Emma. "What are you guys doing here?"

Emma looked sheepish. "We had to tell Sophie the truth."

"The *whole* truth?" Olivia asked nervously.

"Yes, Olivia," Sophie said. "I know you didn't want to worry me. But you should have said something."

"I'm sorry," Olivia apologized. "I just thought that we'd tell you *after* we found Henry. We heard a message from him last night. He's at Demon Falls."

"Wait a minute," Stephanie said. "If we're all here, then who's at home doing wedding prep?"

Emma eyed a flowering bush nearby. "We can do it here!" she said excitedly. "These flowers will make the perfect bridal bouquet—especially because Sophie and Henry work together at the Animal Rescue Station."

"A tropical-themed wedding . . ." Stephanie said thoughtfully.

Sophie smiled. "I love that idea! Now, let's find the groom, shall we?"

"We'll find him," Olivia assured her aunt. "I wonder if

I can see Demon Falls from here."

She used her binoculars to look up the river.
Through the lenses, she couldn't quite see the
falls. But she did see something else—a log
bobbing wildly down the rushing river. And a
baby panda was clinging to it! He was in danger!

"Bamboo!" Olivia cried with a gasp.

Emma was still thinking about the wedding.
"Bamboo, yeah," she said, picking up a tall stalk of
bamboo from the ground. "We could use this—"

"Great idea, Emma." Olivia snatched the

bamboo stalk out of her friend's hand.

"For decoration," Emma finished, blinking in confusion as Olivia raced to the water's edge.

The friends rushed alongside the river as Bamboo continued to bob in and out of the water. He looked terrified!

"This river leads to a waterfall!" Sophie exclaimed. "We've got to save him!"

Olivia spotted a large log overhanging the water a little way downstream. That gave her a clever idea.

Quickly, the girls and Sophie jumped onto the log. Bamboo was coming at them fast! Olivia held the bamboo stalk down over the water so the panda could see it. She knew that pandas ate mostly bamboo. They only had one chance to save the poor cub. Hopefully, his instincts would kick in and he would reach for the tasty-looking stalk.

Just in the nick of time, Bamboo spotted the stalk. His eyes lit up, and he licked his lips. When he was close enough, he chomped on the bamboo with his teeth! With help from her friends, Olivia pulled the little cub to safety.

"We did it!" she cried.

Bamboo looked grateful to be back on dry land. But the little cub held his stomach and grimaced.

"Come here, Bamboo," Sophie said gently. She examined the little panda. "His abdomen is very tender. I need to take him back to the rescue station."

"I'll call Matthew," Stephanie offered.

Sophie nodded. "I'll stay with the cub until Matthew gets here. You girls go ahead and find Henry."

"Okay," Olivia said. "We'll call you when we get there."

Andrea patted the panda cub. "Feel better, Bamboo."

The friends looked at one another worriedly. The jungle was a dangerous place. Hopefully, wherever Henry was, he wasn't in the same sort of situation!

Chapter 5:
Demon Falls

Hours later, the girls were still trekking in search of Demon Falls. Mia glanced at the sky. It would be dark soon, and they were still no closer to finding Henry.

"Demon Falls should be right here according to the map," Olivia said, looking around.

Mia sighed. "But it's not."

"Does anyone else get the feeling we're being watched?" Andrea asked, sounding nervous.

Suddenly, something leaped out of the trees and landed on her arm! Andrea cried out.

"Get it off me!" she yelled.

Mia recognized what the creature was and giggled. "Andrea, it's just a chameleon."

"Huh?" Andrea blinked at the small lizard. It looked up at her and promptly changed color to match her shirtsleeve. "Oh, hey there," Andrea said. "Do you have a name?" The chameleon cocked his head at her. "I think you look like a Tony. That's what I'll call you," Andrea said.

Meanwhile, Olivia studied her map.

"Come on, you guys," she said. "I think Demon Falls is this way."

Mia raised an eyebrow doubtfully. Olivia had been saying that all day! But each time they had followed her, the girls ended up more lost than before.

"Why don't we ask Tony?" Andrea suggested. "He's a local. Tony, do you know where Demon Falls is?"

The chameleon seemed to understand. He began leaping from branch to branch—in the opposite direction from the way Olivia had been pointing.

"You guys, that's not right!" Olivia exclaimed as the others followed the lizard. "Demon Falls should be this way!"

But Olivia turned out to be wrong. Following the little chameleon's lead, the girls soon heard the roar of water and then emerged into a clearing at the base of a large waterfall. They'd finally reached Demon Falls!

Olivia glanced at her map, embarrassed. "Well, at least we're here." Then she called out in a loud voice, "Henry! Are you here? Henry!"

But nobody answered.

"I don't see any footprints," Stephanie said. "Or a leftover campfire."

"It doesn't look like anyone has been here in a while," Mia agreed. She shivered as a wild animal's shriek echoed in the distance. "Or maybe whoever comes here never comes back."

"Don't joke, Mia." Emma's face was pale. "This place is already giving me a creepy vibe!"

Suddenly, the girls' walkie-talkie crackled to life. Olivia pressed a button. "Henry?" she asked hopefully.

"It's Sophie, Olivia," a voice replied through heavy static from the speaker. "You haven't found Henry yet?"

"Not yet," Olivia told her. "But we will, I promise! We're losing light, so we'll have to set up camp for the night."

"We will?" Emma sounded worried. "Here?"

"*Shh,*" Olivia shushed her. Then she spoke into the walkie-talkie again. "We'll call you back when we find him. How's Bamboo?"

"He's going to be just fine," Sophie said.

Mia and the other girls sighed in relief. "Okay," Olivia said. "We'll call you later. Over."

As soon as Olivia had signed off, Emma piped up. "We can't stay here all night!"

"There's no time to argue, Emma," Olivia insisted. "We need to collect wood for a campfire."

"But—" Emma protested.

"A fire will keep wild animals away, Emma," Mia told her.

"Oh!" Emma's eyes widened. She looked around and began grabbing twigs off the ground. "Then here's a branch. And here. And here's another one!"

The girls giggled. "Oh, Emma."

A short while later, the sun sank low beneath the treetops. Dusk fell over the jungle, draping everything in thick shadow. But the girls' campfire crackled merrily, lighting up the clearing with a comforting glow. Together, they unpacked the camping food they'd brought in their backpacks and warmed it up. All around them, the jungle seemed very dark and scary. But as long as they were together, none of them felt too frightened.

"Nice fire," Stephanie said, holding out her hands.

"Yeah," Olivia agreed. "And look at the stars."

Mia sighed. "Beautiful."

Andrea dropped her fork into her bowl with a loud clang. "Okay, but this camping food tastes terrible!"

"Can't argue with that," Emma said.

Stephanie groaned, pushing her food away. "Speaking of food, tonight was supposed to be the cake tasting for the wedding."

Olivia shook her head. "Let's just make the best of it. All that matters is that we find Henry."

Suddenly, another animal cry erupted somewhere in the jungle. Emma jumped.

"I really don't like it here," she said.

"Emma," Andrea said, "those sounds are just—"

"Spooky?" Emma asked.

"No." Andrea shook her head. "It's the jungle singing to you. Listen!"

Mia smiled. Andrea always had a unique way of looking at things. The jungle noises really *did* sound like singing! That inspired the five girls to start singing themselves. And singing together made them all feel much better!

Well, almost all of them. Mia noticed Olivia wandering over to pick up her map again, and she followed.

"It's not your fault, you know," Mia told Olivia. "You're doing the best you can to find Henry."

Olivia sighed. "Really? Leading us all in a circle? Thinking the others were wild animals? Nearly missing Demon Falls altogether?"

"Don't be so hard on yourself," Mia said.

"I won't," Olivia replied. This time she sounded determined. "Not once we find him, that is." She peered at the map and blinked. "*Hmm*, what's that place?"

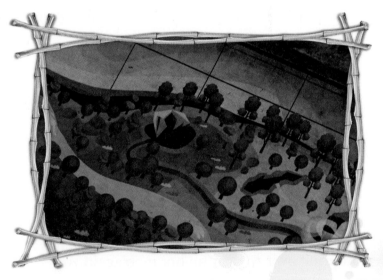

She pointed to a spot on the map. It showed a drawing of a large rock along with some other markings. The rock also had a waterfall leading away from it. But there was no name.

"Let's ask Matthew if he knows," Mia suggested.

Olivia called Matthew on the walkie-talkie. "There's another waterfall on the map north of the gorge," she told him. "It has little diamond shapes by it. Do you know what it is?"

"It doesn't have a name," Matthew said. "But most people call it Diamond Falls. Rumor has it there are diamonds there, but no one's ever found any."

"Thanks, Matthew," Olivia said. She signed off and stared into space thoughtfully for a moment. "Diamond Falls . . ." she murmured. "Demon Falls . . ." She gasped. "That's it!"

Chapter 6: Jungle Rescue!

The other girls gathered around Olivia. She was so excited she could hardly get the words out.

"Henry didn't say he was at *Demon* Falls," she said hurriedly. "I think he said he was at *Diamond* Falls! I bet he went there looking for a diamond for the wedding!"

Mia gasped. "That totally makes sense!"

"We'll head for Diamond Falls first thing in the morning," Stephanie declared. "Good work, Olivia!"

Bright and early, the girls trekked through the

jungle again. It didn't take them long to reach their new destination.

Olivia knew as soon as she saw it that it had to be Diamond Falls. A wide flow of water gushed down over a rock surface. And jagged, diamond-shaped stones stuck out near the top.

Suddenly, Olivia spotted something on the ground that made her gasp.

"A walkie-talkie!" she cried. She looked frantically around the base of the falls. "Henry? Henry!"

Tony the chameleon was riding on Andrea's head. He unexpectedly leaped down to her arm and let out a frightened chirp.

"What is it, Tony?" Andrea asked. She followed the chameleon's gaze and gulped. "Uh, guys?"

The girls looked where Andrea was staring and their jaws dropped. A tiger was just a few hundred feet from them! The huge creature paced across a

rocky ledge near the top of the falls.

"I see her," Olivia said nervously.

Just then, there was a shout from above.
"Olivia! Up here!"

The girls gasped. It was Henry! He was
trapped on a rocky outcropping jutting from the
middle of the rushing falls!

"Henry!" Olivia exclaimed. "Thank goodness
we found you!"

She was overjoyed to see Henry safe and
sound! But her happiness was short-lived. Olivia

quickly realized that Henry was trapped. There was no way he could jump far enough to reach the closest ledge, and Olivia wasn't sure he'd want to, since that was where the tiger was pacing. The outcropping was also far too high for him to leap down into the river below. That meant Henry was in great danger.

Meanwhile, Henry held something up. Olivia squinted to see what it was. "A tiny tiger cub!" she cried.

"We need to get this cub to her mother," Henry called. "She's very weak!"

"But what about you? How do we get you down?" Olivia called back.

"You've got to stop the waterfall," Henry shouted. "The mechanism for the dam is up over those rocks."

Mia pointed. "Look, there's a path. It must lead to the top of the dam."

The girls hurried up the path. Soon Olivia,

Mia, and Stephanie were inspecting the dam mechanism. A large wooden wheel controlled the door that slid closed to block the waterfall. But the wheel was stuck, and there weren't any spokes to turn it.

"It's broken," Olivia said. "But I think we can fix it."

Mia nodded. "If we can find tree branches just the right size . . ."

"Then we can use them to replace the broken spokes," Olivia finished. "Great idea, Mia!"

Quickly, the girls scouted the area near the river. There were many branches, but most were too big, too small, too crooked, or just not quite right.

Finally, Mia found a few that looked perfect. "I think these will work."

Mia, Emma, and Andrea used the dam's pulley system to hoist the branches up to Olivia and Stephanie. Together, the two of them wedged the branches tightly into place.

"Okay," Olivia said. "Fingers crossed that it works!"

She grabbed the branch handles and pushed the wheel. Very slowly, the wheel groaned and began to turn. As it did, the dam door rolled out across the river. Finally, it reached the other side, cutting off the flow of water completely!

"It worked!" Stephanie cried.

"Great job, Olivia!" Henry called as the girls whooped with joy.

Olivia ran out into the dry riverbed and looked down at the outcropping where Henry was standing. Now it would be easy to pull him up to safety!

But there was still another problem to solve. "We have to get the cub to her mother!" she called down to Henry.

The mother tiger's ledge was still too far to jump—even for a tiger. And Olivia couldn't see any way to reach it from the top of the cliff, either. Would the girls have to hike through the jungle in search of whatever path the tiger had taken to get there? Or . . .

"I know!" Emma shouted from the bottom of the cliff. "We can use my backpack!"

At first Olivia wasn't sure what her friend meant, but when Emma explained, it made perfect sense. The girls had already set up the pulley system to get the tree branches up the cliff to fix the dam mechanism. With just a

few adjustments, they rigged it to carry Emma's backpack straight past Henry's ledge *and* the ledge where the mother tiger waited. Quickly, the girls hoisted up Emma's backpack. Henry carefully tucked the cub into the sturdy pack.

"There you go," he said. "Okay, Olivia!"

Olivia and Stephanie fed out the pulley line, being careful not to jostle the cub. Moments later, the backpack touched down on the ledge in front of the mother tiger.

The cub leaped out with an excited little whimper. The mother tiger nuzzled it. Even from where they were standing, Olivia and the others could hear the tigers purring happily as they were reunited.

"It worked!" Olivia exclaimed as her friends cheered and high-fived one another.

"Nicely done, girls!" Henry said once Olivia and Stephanie had pulled him to safety at the top of the cliff.

Now that her soon-to-be uncle was rescued, Olivia had a few questions for him. "How in the world did you get trapped there?"

"Well, I heard the tiger cub whimpering from behind the waterfall," Henry explained. "So I started to cross the rock bridge to get to her. The mother tiger pounced on the bridge behind me, and the bridge began to crumble under my feet."

He pointed, and Olivia noticed something. The shapes of the outcropping and the ledge looked like two ends of a narrow stone bridge—

with only the middle part missing!

"I jumped one way, and the mother tiger jumped the other," Henry continued. "That's how I got trapped with the cub."

Olivia was amazed. What a close call! She was glad that everyone was all right. And she wasn't the only one.

"I know someone who's going to be *so* happy to see you!" she told Henry with a smile.

Chapter 7:
Reunited

All the way back to base camp, the friends sang songs, told stories, and tried to spot interesting birds in the treetops. Tony the chameleon rode on Andrea's head, and the girls giggled every time he snapped his long tongue to snatch an insect out of the air.

Still, the friends didn't dawdle. They'd used the walkie-talkie to call and let Sophie and Matthew know that they were on their way. The girls could hear the relief in Sophie's voice when they said they'd found Henry.

Sure enough, when they reached the edge of the camp, Sophie and Matthew hurried out to meet them. As soon as she spotted Henry, Sophie started running.

Henry swept Sophie into his arms and twirled her around in a giant hug. Both of them were smiling from ear to ear.

Two baby pandas came tumbling out to greet the group, also. It was Shadow and Bamboo. Bamboo looked just as healthy as Shadow now! Stephanie and Olivia picked up the cubs and cuddled them.

Meanwhile, Sophie and Henry couldn't stop gazing into each other's eyes. "I'm so glad you're okay!" Sophie said quietly.

"Me, too," Henry replied, brushing hair away from Sophie's forehead.

Emma sighed. It was all so romantic!

"Welcome back." Matthew walked up to them. He looked relieved to have his uncle back safe and sound, too.

"Thanks, Matthew," Henry said. "Glad to be back. Lucky for me, the girls are great at rescue missions." He winked at the five friends.

"You can say that again!" Matthew nodded. "But what were you doing out at Diamond Falls? No one's ever found any diamonds there."

A gleam came to Henry's eye. "Not until now!"
Everyone gasped as he pulled out a large,
unpolished stone from his pocket. It was the
biggest diamond the friends had ever seen! The
girls couldn't believe it. Henry had found a real
diamond at Diamond Falls!

"I thought this might make a nice wedding
ring," he said to Sophie.

Emma clasped her hands. "Oh! *So* romantic!"

Sophie looked thrilled. "It *is* romantic," she agreed. "And I love it. But most of all, I love you. And I have an even better idea."

"You do?" Henry asked.

Sophie nodded. Now she had a gleam in her eye. "I know how much this Animal Rescue Station means to you. After all the hard work you've done to build it, what would make me happiest of all is if we use the money from this diamond to benefit the station. Think how many more animals we could help!"

Henry seemed surprised. "Are you sure?" he asked. "It's a wonderful idea, but I want you to be happy, too. Won't you want a wedding ring?"

Sophie nodded. "I'm sure," she said. "And with the money left over, we could buy a smaller ring. That way, whenever I wear it, I'll think of you and all the wonderful things you've accomplished— for both of us."

Henry grinned broadly. He pulled Sophie in to a loving hug. "If that's what you want, of course," he told his bride-to-be.

Emma smiled. "It's still romantic," she announced.

Her friends all giggled. They definitely couldn't argue with that!

Chapter 8:
Wedding Belles

A few weeks later, the day of the wedding dawned bright and clear—another perfect Heartlake City morning.

Olivia and her friends arrived at the wedding venue early. The cake was already there, looking scrumptious. Stephanie had overseen the baking process, and Emma had arranged the topping of tropical fruits with her usual artistic flair.

All five friends had helped decorate the outdoor tent with palm fronds, bamboo, and colorful flowers.

"It's our own little piece of the jungle right here for our wedding!" Sophie exclaimed happily when she saw the decorations. "How can I thank you girls for all you've done?"

Olivia smiled. "We promised your big day would be perfect!"

Soon the guests began to arrive. Everyone was in a festive mood. Matthew looked very handsome in his suit and tie. And Olivia, Mia, Emma, Andrea, and Stephanie were bridesmaids.

Their dresses were all the same style, except that Sophie had let each girl choose the color she liked best. Emma had picked a bright pink shade that set off her long, dark hair. Andrea had decided on a vibrant yellow that matched her outgoing personality. Mia's dress was the perfect tint of green to complement her eyes. And Stephanie had chosen a bright, beautiful red.

Olivia thought all her friends looked terrific— and she felt just as beautiful in her coral dress.

But nobody looked as perfect as Sophie in her gorgeous white wedding gown. The sparkle in her eyes shone even brighter than her jeweled tiara.

Everyone watched delightedly as she walked down the aisle to meet her handsome groom. In a heartfelt ceremony, the couple traded vows and became husband and wife.

And then, it was time for the party! Everyone wanted to celebrate the newly married couple.

Servers came around with silver trays piled high with hors d'oeuvres—delicious appetizers and treats all with a jungle theme!

Meanwhile, a table decorated with beautiful jungle flowers held rows of tall, sparkling glasses. Guests lined up to each pour themselves a refreshing glass of fruity tropical punch from a glimmering crystal pitcher.

Later, Sophie and Henry danced their first dance together as husband and wife. All the guests watched happily as the bride and groom shared such a special moment.

And then, everyone joined them on the dance floor! Matthew deejayed and kept the party going with awesome beats. Olivia and her friends had a wonderful time bopping and dancing to the jamming music.

A short while later, Andrea had a special surprise planned for the bride and groom. She took the stage to sing a beautiful song she had written just for the occasion:

This is the best day of my whole life.
Now everything's good and the world feels right
'cause you're here by my side.
Even when we're in the wildest place,
it's just adventure, don't be afraid.
I'll be by your side.
We'll make it through!
Together we can never ever lose.
Forever us!

The party continued well into the night, with colorful string lights twinkling as brightly as stars overhead. Olivia was sure her aunt and uncle were going to live happily ever after.

And as for her and her friends? This was the perfect ending to one of their most exciting adventures yet!